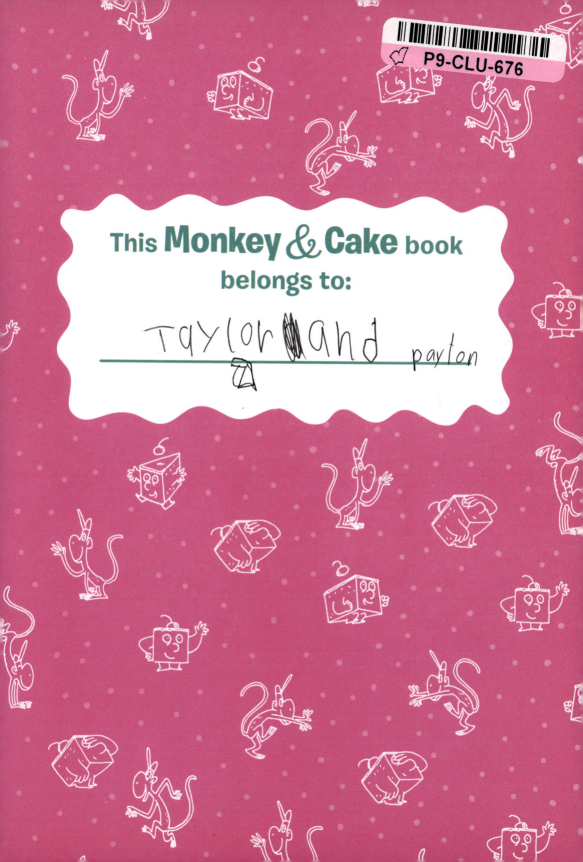

This **Monkey** & **Cake** book
belongs to:

Taylor and payton

To Lance & Derek, friendship is priceless –D.D.

My technique is a mix of dark pencils and acrylic.
I use watercolor brushes with marten hairs and paper with no grain,
usually Sennelier or Arches 300g.
–Olivier Tallec

Text copyright © 2019 by Drew Daywalt
Illustrations copyright © 2019 by Olivier Tallec

Library of Congress Cataloging-in-Publication Data available
ISBN 978-1-338-14388-1

10 9 8 7 6 5 4 3 2 1 • 19 20 21 22 23
Printed in China   62
First edition, September 2019
The text type and the display type was set in Burbank. • Book design by Jess Tice-Gilbert

a **Monkey & Cake** book

My Tooth Is LOST!

Written by **Drew Daywalt** • Illustrated by **Olivier Tallec**

Orchard Books
New York
An Imprint of Scholastic Inc.

You lost a tooth?
But that is
not a bad thing.
That is a **good** thing.

It is a **good** thing
that I lost a tooth?

How is it a **good** thing
that I lost a tooth?

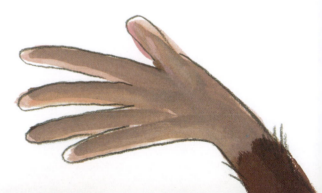

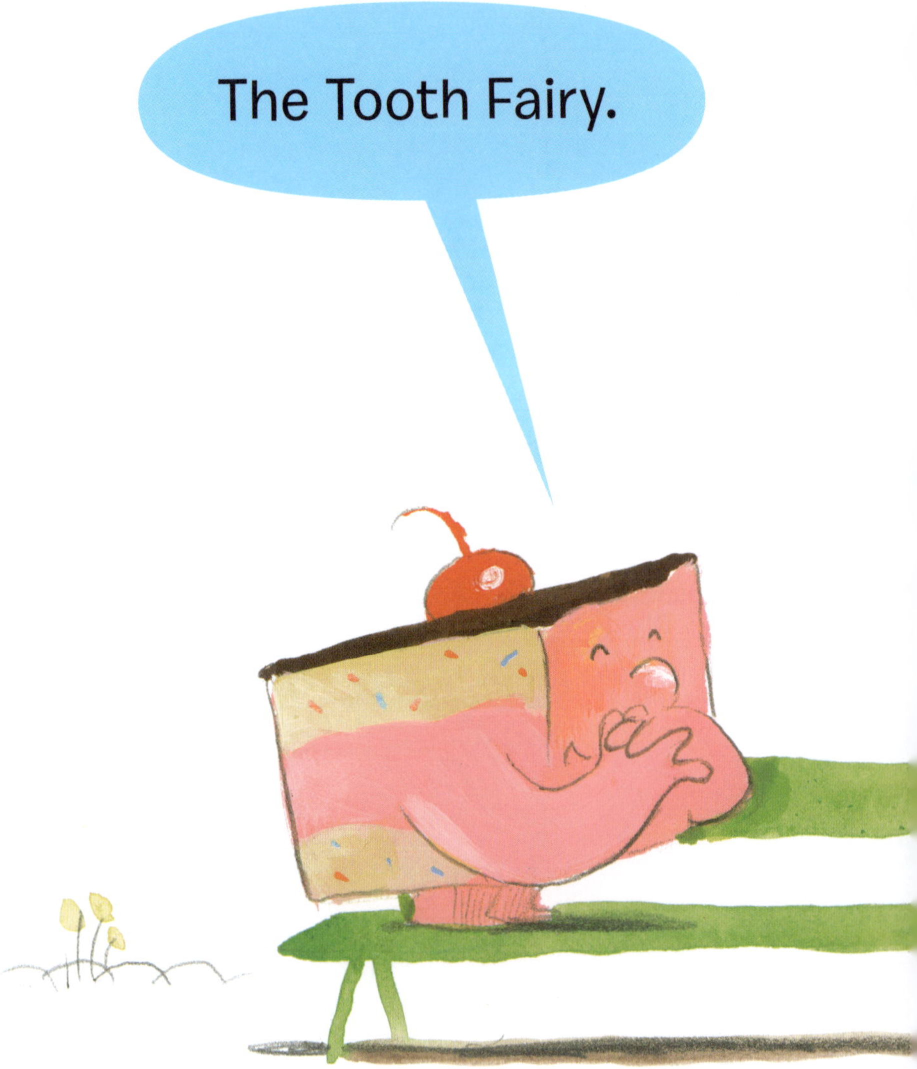
The Tooth Fairy.

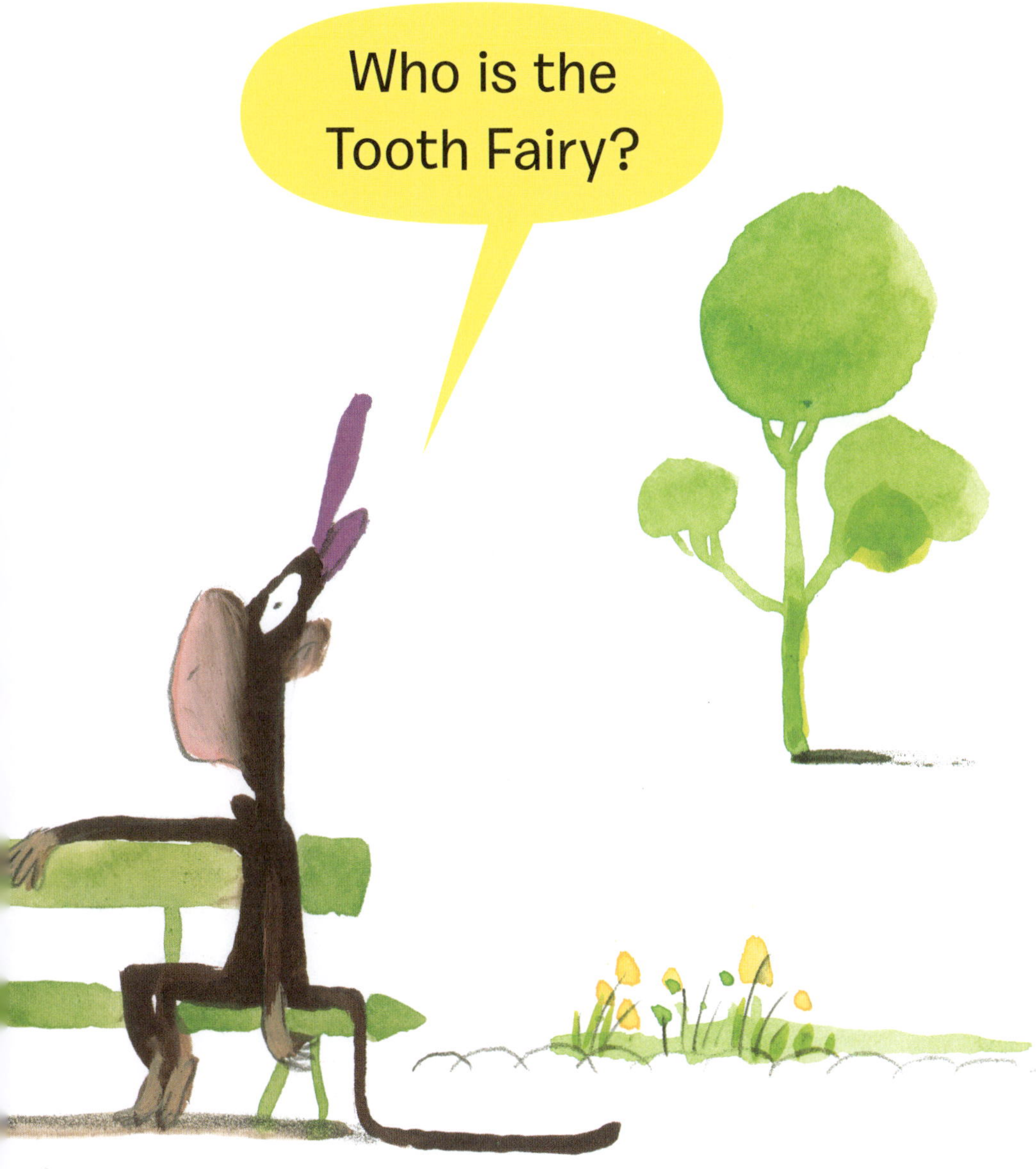
Who is the Tooth Fairy?

You don't know who the Tooth Fairy is?

The Tooth Fairy is the one who comes and takes your lost tooth.

Wait.

Are you saying my
tooth is not lost?
It is **stolen**?

This Tooth Fairy
stole my tooth
and now it is **gone**?

No no no no no . . .
When you lose a tooth,
you put it under your pillow at night,
and when you wake up
the tooth is gone.

I do not know.

But if you put the tooth under your pillow, the Tooth Fairy will take it and leave you money.

What if I like the tooth?
What if I like the tooth
and want to keep it?

Then you won't get any money.

Because I **found** my lost tooth. See?

There he is. Hi, Kevin.
His name is Kevin.
Where were you?
I was lost.
Well, welcome back.